GET INTO
citizenship

Crime and legal awareness

Contents

How your work will be assessed

There is a single end of key stage descriptor for citizenship:

'The expectations match the level of demand in other subjects and are broadly equivalent to Levels 5 and 6 at key stage 3.'

Each scheme of work states what 'most' students should achieve (ie. Level 5), that 'some pupils have not made so much progress' (ie. Level 4) and that 'some pupils have progressed further' (ie. Level 6).

Most of the activities that you complete in this book will be graded to either Level 4, 5 or 6. The chart below gives you an idea of what you will have to do to achieve each level.

End of key stage descriptor for citizenship (broken into three strands)	Level 4 'some pupils have not made so much progress'	Level 5 'most pupils'	Level 6 'some pupils have progressed further'
Strand 1 *'have a broad knowledge and understanding of the topical events they study; the rights, responsibilities and duties of citizens; the role of the voluntary sector; forms of government, provision of public services; and the criminal and legal systems'*	Pupils will know what it means to commit a crime and are aware that young children are immune from criminal prosecution. They will understand what voting is and some of the things that MPs do. They will know some of the differences between local and national government.	Pupils can describe how the law treats people and understand the function of parliament and democratic processes both at national and local level. They understand the basic structure of the youth justice system. They can conduct an enquiry and use the findings to draw simple conclusions.	Pupils know the importance of rights in a fair trial and they can explain and evaluate alternative voting systems. They reflect on how media coverage can influence elections. They understand the legal and ethical responsibilities of local government. They research, analyse and interpret data and use this to deliver presentations.
Strand 2 *'show understanding of how the public gets information; how opinion is formed and expressed, including through the media; and how and why changes take place in society'*	Pupils can give reasons for and results of events and changes and combine information from sources to answer questions.	Pupils begin to show how processes cause similarity and differences between different places and different environments. They begin to make links between reasons and changes and to evaluate evidence to reach a conclusion.	Pupils are able to explain why there are different interpretations of the same event and they gather and use evidence critically to show how and why opinions are formed and the different effects that various types of information have on people.
Strand 3 *'take part in school and community-based activities, demonstrating personal and group responsibility in their attitudes to themselves and others'*	Pupils talk and listen with confidence in an increasing range of contexts. They describe events and convey opinions. They ask questions and respond to the views of others.	In discussion they pay close attention to what others say, ask questions to develop ideas and make contributions that take account of others' views. Their talk engages the interest of the listener.	Pupils adapt their talk to the demands of different contexts. They use a variety of vocabulary and expression. They are fluent in their use of standard English.

Know your rights

What do you know?

- What do we mean by human rights?
- What are civil rights?

What will you know?

By the end of this unit you will know

- the difference between human rights and civil rights
- how difficult it sometimes is to tell them apart
- about the idea of responsibility.

Rights for everyone?

Everyone should have the right to live a full and happy life. In this unit we shall be looking at what 'rights' mean, and whether it's really true that everybody should be free to do just what they want.

Not everyone can live in peace, and often it's necessary to protect those who are affected by wars or by harsh leaders who care little for other people. In 1948 the United Nations drew up a long list of basic rights that they felt everyone should live by – the **Universal Declaration of Human Rights** – and since then there have been several others, such as the **European Convention on Human Rights** 1950, and in Britain, the **Human Rights Act** 1998. In 1989, UNICEF issued the **Convention on the Rights of the Child**, designed to protect children everywhere. The trouble is that writing a list is one thing, but making everybody in the world follow it is quite another. There are three main problems.

- Not everybody agrees on what is right or wrong.
- Some leaders choose to ignore human rights to suit what they want to do.
- Sometimes giving one person a right may cause problems for others.

When World War II ended in 1945, many of the world's nations formed an organisation that would work to keep world peace, and the United Nations first met in New York in 1946. Later, they added UNICEF – a section dedicated to the welfare of children all round the world.

① ▷ Problems with rights

This activity will help you to decide why there might be problems with giving everybody equal rights.

Here are some extracts from the Human Rights Act that is used in Britain. Write each one in a table. Next to it fill in why the rights might be good, but also what problems there might be. The first one has been started for you. See if you can add anything to it.

The Human Rights Act 1998

In 1998, the Labour government led by Tony Blair introduced the Human Rights Act. It is based on another document, the European Convention on Human Rights, and sets out in writing for the first time a list of basic human rights that all citizens of Great Britain should enjoy.

Article 9 Everyone has a right to freedom of thought, conscience and religion.

Article 10 Everyone has the right to freedom of expression (saying or writing what they want).

Article 11 Everyone has the right to freedom of peaceful assembly (protest marches, for example).

IT'S OK. THEY'RE JUST ARGUING ABOUT THEIR RIGHT TO ARGUE ABOUT THEIR RIGHTS.

Human right	Good	Problems?
Article 9	People should be allowed to believe what they want.	What if they believe that you should be harmed?
Article 10		
Article 11		

Now discuss your list with others in the class, and see how much they agree or disagree with you. If you find that some of your classmates think you're wrong, that tells you just how difficult it is to make a list of rights that everybody will want to follow all the time.

How your work will be assessed

As you go through the units in this book, you will be able to see at which level you're working. For this assessment, these are the kind of things you will have to do to reach particular levels.

Level 4

You've thought of a few reasons on both sides, and can argue about why you've thought of them. You might be able to give a few examples to prove your case.

Level 5

You've listened to other people's arguments, and discussed with them why they might be right or wrong. You've taken that into account when you filled in the table.

Level 6

You've done what Level 5 says, but also used real examples that you've found out. You may have realised that some of these rights might have to be changed in certain circumstances, and said a little about why that might be difficult.

Human rights and civil rights

Most will agree that human rights are a good thing to have. When we live with other people, however, it is not always an easy matter to decide what rights to allow, and what rights to stop. Often, a lot of the rights that we enjoy are rights that are given to us by our governments, and they can be very different in different countries.

In Britain, for example, we can be sold alcohol in a public bar when we are 18 years old, but in the United States, the age is 21. In Britain we would like to have the human right

to say what we like, but we might soon find that if we criticise people in public those people could take us to court.

So each country has rules for its own citizens, and we call those **civil rights**. If they seem to agree with human rights so much the better, but if governments ignore human rights when they make up their rules, then there will be problems for the citizens of those countries.

© Peter Turnley/Corbis

In June 1989 in Beijing, many peaceful protestors were killed by the troops of the Chinese government for demonstrating. They wanted to live according to democracy, as countries like Britain and America do. The government ordered its troops to open fire, and nobody knows how many were killed or imprisoned, but it is probably thousands.

In China, people did not have the civil right to demonstrate like this, but was this also against the human rights of the people?

❷ What is the difference between civil and human rights?

An activity to help you to understand the difference between civil and human rights.

What to do

Here is a list of possible rights. Try to decide which ones are human rights, which everybody is entitled to, and which ones are civil rights, granted by the government to its citizens. Think these through carefully, and write down your answer. They're not as easy as they might look. Then, discuss with others why some of them may not be seen as human rights in Britain. What kinds of problems might there be if they were?

- **The right to a fair trial**

- **The right to a job**

- **The right to leave school at 16**

- **The right not to be tortured**

- **The right to get married without parents' permission at 18**

- **The right to freedom of religion**

Responsibilities
You've probably discovered that it's often difficult to tell the difference between human and civil rights. When a government allows you to have rights, it comes at a price. With rights come **responsibilities**, things that you are expected to do in return. That's what we'll look at in the next unit.

What is law?

What do you know?

- What are 'laws' and where do they come from?

- Why do we need them?

What will you know?

By the end of this unit you will know

- why we need laws

- where our laws come from

- how laws are made.

Key words: responsibility, statute law, common law, case law, European law, custom, judicial precedent.

A world without law

Imagine your class working quietly. Your teacher suddenly says, 'Right, I'm going out of the room for ten minutes, and during that time you can do anything you like. You won't be punished, whatever you do.' Suddenly you have a room without laws. What do you think would happen? Would students in the room be harmed by others, or have their property taken?

Hopefully, most students would care about their friends enough not to do anything wrong, but there's always a chance that somebody might do something that would break the normal rules. That's one of the reasons we have laws, however nice we think

people are. We try to give citizens as many civil rights as possible, but the government has a duty to see that

- society remains peaceful and prosperous
- innocent people are not harmed
- society is as fair as possible.

The government also has to ask people to do things that they might not always want to do. We call these **responsibilities**, and we accept them in return for being trusted enough to enjoy civil rights. The alternative would be a huge set of strict laws that made sure that everybody always did as they were told. As citizens, we might not like that.

 1 ▶ What are rights and what are responsibilities?

An activity to help you understand the nature of responsibility in society.

We're going to see that being a citizen with rights means that we have certain duties to live up to.

Right	Responsibility
The right to freedom of speech.	*Not to say anything that might unjustly damage the reputation of others.*
	Not to say anything that might put other citizens in danger.
	Not to say anything that might be insulting racially.
	Not to say anything that might lead others to break the law.
The right to freedom of movement.	
The right to freedom of worship.	
The right to demonstrate peacefully.	
The right to decide what subjects you take in Year 10.	
The right to drive a car at 17.	

What to do

Copy the table, and for each of the rights, write an explanation of the responsibility that might go with it, if it is to work properly. The first one has been done for you, but you could probably add to it. Discuss your answers with others.

Laws

If everybody always agreed on what to do, people could probably be left to decide for themselves on most issues. The trouble is that this never happens, and that's why we need laws. Laws are there to do several things.

- To make sure society remains peaceful and as fair as possible (to make sure we live up to our responsibilities).

- To settle disputes.

- To protect us.

- To tell us what we are supposed to do and not to do (our responsibilities).

How we get our law

In some countries, law was written down almost in one go, and changed over time as necessary. Britain has not done that, and our laws have grown over the centuries.

The prime minister, Tony Blair, speaks during a debate in the House of Commons.

Where we get our laws from

Parliament is the main law-making body in the United Kingdom. The laws it passes are called **statutes.**

Laws and regulations of the **European Union**. Since 1973, we have agreed to accept some of these rules and they usually have to be followed.

Common law
Our laws have grown over the centuries as times have changed. If these laws clash with statute law, then statute law is followed.

LAW

Case law
Over the centuries, judges have had to make decisions about what the law means. Gradually this has led to new decisions that are usually followed by other courts. This is called **judicial precedent**.

Custom
Occasionally, if something has been happening unopposed for long enough, then it can have the force of law, as long as no offence is committed. This is getting less important.

❷ ➤ An activity to find out where our law comes from

In this activity, you will be able to see where the law comes from, and look in more detail at the most important type of law – law made by Parliament.

Written laws that affect the whole nation are made by Parliament, and only Parliament can change those laws. While the proposed law is going through Parliament, it is called a bill, and when it becomes law, it is called an Act of Parliament. Remember that a law applies to you even if you don't know about it!

You will need
- **Research materials such as newspaper archives and access to the Internet.**

What to do

Look at the diagram at the right. It shows how a law goes through Parliament. Now research a particular bill that has recently gone through this process and become law – or been rejected. Find out as much as you can about it. Who put it forward? Who opposed it?

You may wish to use newspaper archives or the Internet – there is useful information on Parliament's website at www.explore.parliament.uk.

How law goes through Parliament

Starts with an idea, or from pressure by the public, or a need to change things.

The government discusses the idea and might issue

a Green Paper (general proposals and discussions) or a White Paper (more detailed proposals)

Very rarely, a private person might introduce a bill

Sometimes, an MP might introduce a bill on their own

House of Commons
First Reading
Not a debate, just introducing the bill.

▼

Second Reading
The bill has been printed. It is explained and questions are asked. A vote is taken.

▼

Committee stage
Going through the bill in detail.

▼

Report stage
Reporting back to the House of Commons.

▼

Third Reading
Bill accepted or rejected – not usually changed much.

→ Bill goes to the House of Lords

House of Lords
Same stages as Commons.

Can either accept it, or change parts, and send it back to the House of Commons. The Lords can only reject the bill for one year.

▼

House of Commons either accepts the changes or gives reasons why it does not.

▼

When agreement has finally been reached, the bill goes to the monarch for Royal Assent.

The bill becomes law (an Act of Parliament).

What is a crime?

What do you know?

- What's the difference between a rule and a law?

- Do crimes always have a victim?

What will you know?

By the end of this unit you will know

- the difference between laws and simple rules

- the difference between civil law and criminal law

- whether laws are always fair to everyone

- whether 'victimless' crimes are possible.

Rules vs laws

'It really is a crime to do that!' 'You're acting like a criminal!' We've all heard expressions like these, and they often mean different things. You can probably tell that there's a difference between simple rules and laws, but can you think exactly what it is?

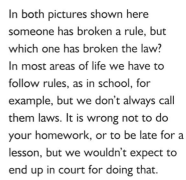

In both pictures shown here someone has broken a rule, but which one has broken the law? In most areas of life we have to follow rules, as in school, for example, but we don't always call them laws. It is wrong not to do your homework, or to be late for a lesson, but we wouldn't expect to end up in court for doing that.

Laws are made to prevent us harming others and ourselves, and to keep order in the country in which we live. We are expected, as citizens, to obey them for the good of everybody, including ourselves.

In Unit 5 you'll learn how people who break the law are dealt with, but for now try to understand that there are two main types of law in this country.

There are the laws that set certain rules for behaviour between individual people or groups, behaviour that everybody else might not be interested in. That is called private law, or **civil law**.

The other type of law is about actions that everybody agrees are wrong no matter who the victim is, and for which the person responsible can be arrested and punished. That is called public law, or **criminal law**, and that's what we'll be discussing here.

Which of these are crimes?

To help you find the difference between crimes, civil law, and things that are just plain wrong.

Look at the events below, and decide which ones are crimes, for which a person could be arrested.

Robbing a petrol station

Lighting a bonfire so that the smoke blows on your neighbour's washing

Taking a day off work to watch a football match

Forging a signature on a cheque

Going to sleep while driving and causing an accident

Refusing to do homework

What to do

Once you've decided which ones are crimes, put the whole list in order of seriousness. Discuss your choice with others in your class. This should give you a better idea of why some actions are called crimes and others are not.

Look at the next example. It shows a cigarette packet, and it's surrounded by laws! One of them, however, is only a general rule, and people wouldn't be arrested if they broke it. Can you see which one? When you do, argue whether you think it should be made into a law, and why.

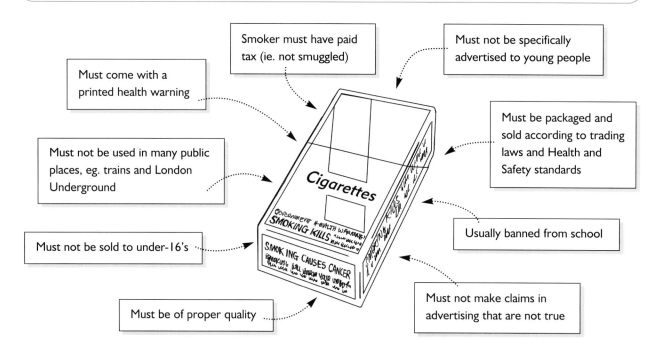

Are laws always fair?

You want to go to the cinema, but your sister wants to go to the park. Your parents decide that you're both going to the park, because you chose where to go last time. They think that's fair, but you don't, because the film won't be on tomorrow, and the park will always be there. It's often the same with laws that are passed for the whole nation. There are so many people living in Britain that many laws cannot always seem fair to everybody all the time. Laws are there for the benefit of as many people as possible – to protect them and to keep the peace.

If a law is seriously out of date, then a new law should be passed to replace it. This often takes a very long time, because not everybody will agree on whether it should happen or not. For example, no woman was allowed to vote until 1918. The law was at last changed because enough people demanded that it should be. Even then, only some women over 30 were allowed to vote, and it was ten more years before that was changed to all women over 21 years old.

❷ ▶ Is it fair?

To discover reasons why some laws are fair, even if they don't always seem so.

What to do

First of all, decide the reasons why some of the laws in the list at the right are saying what they do. Then discuss with a partner whether they should be changed or not. What would be the good or bad effects of that? Remember that doing any of these things at present would be committing a crime, but that criminal law is there to protect others as well as yourselves.

- You can't buy a pet until you're 12 years old.
- Nobody can sell you cigarettes until you're 16 years old.
- Nobody can sell you alcohol until you're 18 years old.
- You can't vote until you're 18 years old.
- You have to be in full-time education until you're 16 years old (notice that the law doesn't say at school!).

And what about these 'can-do' things? Should these be changed?

- You can get married with your parents' permission at 16 years old.
- You can be responsible for a crime at 10 years old.
- You can have a soft drink in a pub unaccompanied at 14 years old.
- You can drive a car at 17.

❸ ▶ Crimes without victims?

This activity will help you to understand that most crimes will harm somebody.

What to do

Read these speech bubbles carefully. Each one shows a different type of crime. In some cases, it's obvious that people are going to get hurt, but in others it might not be so clear. Number each one, and list all the possible victims. Discuss the results with the class, and try to decide whether there is such a thing as a 'victimless' crime. Be sure to give reasons why you're arriving at your answers. Add more to the list if you can. Your teacher will assess your answers. Do you think that all these examples should be called 'crimes'?

'I take illegal drugs. It's my right. No one gets hurt except me.'

'I found a wallet with five pounds in it. I kept it because nobody would have ever known who the owner was. There was no name in it.'

'I'm not harming anybody. I like to drive without a seatbelt and talk on my mobile while I'm driving. It's no one else's business.'

'I robbed a bank. Nobody who used it will lose out. The bank will make up what they've lost. They've got plenty of money.'

Young people and crime

What do you know?

- What sort of crimes do young people commit?
- Are children held responsible for their actions in the same way as adults?

What will you know?

By the end of this unit you will know about

- the age of responsibility
- some of the possible reasons for criminal behaviour in young people.

Age of criminal responsibility

Do you remember how we've learned that responsibility goes hand in hand with rights, and that in return for rights, citizens have certain duties? In England, Wales and Northern Ireland the law says that children under 10 years old do not know what a crime really is, and cannot be held responsible.

It isn't the same in every country. In Ireland, for example, the age is fixed at seven, and in Scotland it's fixed at eight. Until 1998, the law said that children up to 14 might not really understand, but that has now been fixed at 10. Do you think that's too young or even too old? Now we'll learn some facts about youth offending, to see how serious the problem might be. In law, a 'youth' is someone up to 17 years old.

0 ▶ Why do young people commit crimes?

This activity will help you to understand some of the reasons given for offending.

Your views on reasons for criminal behaviour

The illustration on page 13 gives some of the usual explanations for criminal behaviour. Read the two stories below it, and write a short account of why you think they happened. What do you think could have been done to stop them offending? How serious were the actions? Do you have any sympathy with them?

Some explanations for criminal behaviour

Resentment against something or someone

Emotional immaturity

Poverty and unemployment

Pressure from society, eg. the need to own things advertised on TV

Pressure from peers (people of your own age)

The need to be noticed, or even famous

A drug or alcohol habit

Greed

Lack of care and understanding of others

Desire for excitement

Case 1

Christina is 12 years old. She has been living in a happy family with her brothers and sisters, but at school she became friends with a group of girls who had a reputation for getting into trouble outside school. One evening, they were all in the local sweetshop, and Christina saw one of her friends take some sweets from the counter and walk out. Her other friend said that nobody would mind because there were plenty of other sweets there, and the shopkeeper wouldn't miss them. She said that Christina should take some too. Besides, it was expected if they were going to be friends. Christina was nervous, but took the sweets. She took a small bar of chocolate that she didn't even like, and joined her friends outside. On the way home, she threw the chocolate away.

Case 2

Gurdev is 15 years old, and is usually bored at school. He isn't particularly good at his lessons, but gets into very little trouble. His reports say that his work is satisfactory, but lacking enthusiasm. He has few friends, and they seem to find him boring. When he tells them that he wants to be a Formula 1 driver when he leaves school, they usually laugh at him. His parents are rarely in, and do not take much interest in his results. One evening, Gurdev was walking home from school and saw a sports car parked, with a window slightly open. There was a case on the seat, and he broke the window and took it. When he opened it, he discovered that it belonged to his neighbour, a good friend of his father, and there was some money in it. He kept the money and threw the case into a hedge.

How your work will be assessed

Level 4
You will show that you understand what happened and will offer some thoughts on why you think these young people became criminals.

Level 5
You will offer good explanations of why these crimes might have happened, and talk about some of the things that could have been done to prevent them.

Level 6
You will do the things mentioned in Level 5, and might also discuss whether these two crimes are as serious as each other. You might discuss whether the difference in ages between Christina and Gurdev might be important.

How serious is youth offending?

All offending is serious, but society gets especially concerned when young people commit crimes. Can you see why? In the next activity, you will get a chance to think about some recent statistics, and to think about whether youth crime can be avoided. In a recent survey, it was discovered that the average age of offending began at just over 13 for boys and 14 for girls, and that girls were eleven times more likely to be convicted for crimes than they would have been 50 years ago.

Crimes can be linked to the use of drugs, and the need to pay for them. It has been estimated that there are about 130 000 serious drug users of all ages, and that there are over 7 000 people in prison for drug or drug-related offences. An important point is that many of these people started young. Some 20 per cent of 13-year-olds in the UK admitted that they had smoked, and 13 per cent of 15- to 16-year-olds had tried cannabis.

The heartening thing is that many of the crimes of young people are committed by relatively few individuals. Some 25 per cent of recorded offences in the survey were committed by just 3 per cent of offenders, and in the sample 10 per cent of young people who had offended were responsible for nearly half the crimes.

❷ ▶ Interpreting statistics about youth crime

An activity to help you understand some trends in youth offending.

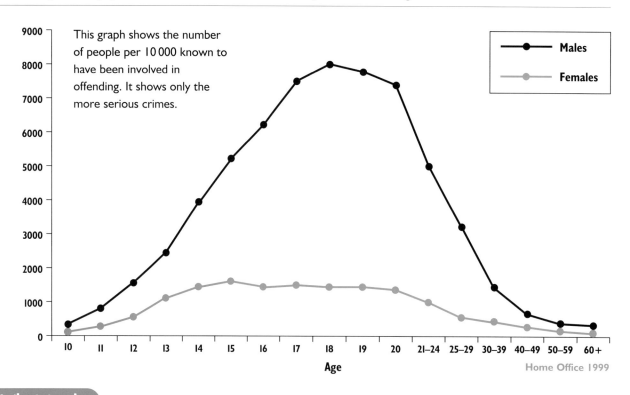

This graph shows the number of people per 10 000 known to have been involved in offending. It shows only the more serious crimes.

Home Office 1999

What to do

This diagram shows that boys commit most crimes by people aged between 10 and 17. In 1999 there were 145 700 known male offenders between the ages of 10 and 17 and 35 000 female offenders. Study the graph carefully, and see whether you can answer the following questions.

1 When does offending by boys reach its worst level?

2 When does this happen for girls?

3 Why do you think the numbers drop so much for boys after this age?

4 Why do you think boys offend so much more than girls?

Bear in mind that the crimes that account for most of these offences are related to theft. Violent crimes against people are comparatively few. If you are working at Levels 5 and 6 you will certainly be able to make some good points to answer questions 3 and 4.

Graphing youth crime figures

This activity will help you to understand in more detail the kind of crimes committed by young people.

Some definitions

Theft – taking something dishonestly with the intention of not giving it back.

Burglary – breaking into property with the intention of committing another crime, like theft.

Robbery – committing theft while using force or the threat of force.

Fraud – making false statements for gain (such as forging someone's signature on a cheque).

You will need

- **Graph paper, coloured pencils and a ruler.**

What to do

The table of figures below shows some of the crimes committed by young people between the ages of 10 and 17 in England and Wales for 1999. You're going to turn these figures into two bar charts. Plan them like the one at the right, and carefully mark the correct figures for males like the one shown in the example.

Then do the same for females, and colour each type of crime by blocks.

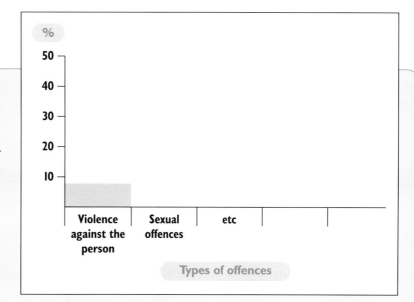

	Males	Females
Violence against the person	8%	8%
Sexual offences	1%	0%
Burglary	9%	3%
Robbery	2%	1%
Theft and handling stolen goods	30%	52%
Fraud and forgery	1%	2%
Criminal damage	3%	1%
Drug offences	8%	3%
Other (excluding motoring)	3%	2%
Motoring	0%	0%
Summary offences (these are much more minor offences, which are dealt with quickly, perhaps at the police station)	35%	28%

Home Office 1999

Now look at the definitions of some of these crimes once more, and see if you can answer the following questions. You might want to use the graphs and the answers to give a short presentation to others in the class.

- Why do you think theft makes up such a large number of crimes?

- List some of the differences between crimes committed by males and females, and try to explain why you think this is so.

- Which of these offences do you think are the most serious, and why?

Good news!
Between 1981 and 1999 there was a drop of 37 per cent in the number of known male youth offenders, and a drop of 15 per cent in the number of female offenders.

4 Analysing youth offending

An activity to help you see in more detail how young people offend at different ages.

What to do

Now you're going to do the same thing in more detail. Here are some figures to show the kind of crimes that young people admitted to doing between 1998 and 1999.

Age	12–13 %	14–15 %	16–17 %	18–21 %	22–25 %	26–30 %	12–30 %
MALES							
Fighting	26	13	36	18	11	3	15
Other violence	16	8	9	3	1	3	5
Buying stolen goods	1	10	16	20	25	20	18
Selling stolen goods	3	4	5	16	4	11	9
Shoplifting	4	15	5	5	5	1	6
Other theft	7	17	17	8	7	3	9
Theft from the workplace	N/A	N/A	1	9	22	15	10
Fraud	N/A	N/A	2	15	21	44	17
Criminal damage	42	34	9	5	3	1	11
All offences	*100*	*100*	*100*	*100*	*100*	*100*	*100*
FEMALES							
Fighting	3	17	9	19	4	0	9
Other violence	0	0	2	0	0	1	1
Buying stolen goods	12	10	48	23	30	25	26
Selling stolen goods	0	1	14	7	4	5	6
Shoplifting	27	41	5	9	5	22	18
Other theft	23	10	7	0	10	1	8
Theft from the workplace	N/A	N/A	4	20	14	6	7
Fraud	N/A	N/A	7	22	25	40	14
Criminal damage	34	21	2	0	8	0	10
All offences	*100*	*100*	*100*	*100*	*100*	*100*	*100*

Home Office 1998–99

Draw two new bar charts for fighting like the one for shoplifting shown here. When you have finished answer the following questions.

- At what age did most males admit to fighting?
- Why do you think the numbers drop off after that?
- How does this compare with females?
- At what age are violent crimes most common among boys? Why do you think this happens?

Kim's case

What do you know?

- What drugs are illegal?
- What are the consequences of using illegal drugs?

What will you know?

By the end of this unit you will

- know some facts about the misuse of drugs
- be able to plan a school campaign that might help those who are in danger of using them.

Drugs

The use of illegal drugs is a serious problem, and though some crimes may not seem to have anything to do with drugs, there is sometimes a connection when an addict commits crime to get money to buy drugs.

The law treats those who buy and sell illegal drugs very seriously, and the penalty for supplying a class A drug can be life imprisonment.

So why do some young people get involved with something that can not only get them into serious trouble with the law, but can also cause so much harm to their bodies, and even kill them?

What the law says

CLASS	EXAMPLES	MAXIMUM PENALTY POSSESSION	MAXIMUM PENALTY SUPPLY
A	Cocaine, ecstasy, LSD, heroin	7 years in prison or fine or both	Life imprisonment
B	Cannabis*, amphetamines	5 years in prison or fine or both	14 years in prison or fine or both
C	Anabolic steroids, tranquillisers	2 years in prison or fine or both	4 years in prison or fine or both

* At the time of publication the government had announced that it planned to make cannabis a class C drug, although this was not yet in effect.

❶ Kim's case

This activity will help you to decide why someone may break the law by possessing drugs, and suggest ways to help prevent it.

What to do

Read through Kim's story, and look carefully at the list of possible reasons why Kim has got herself into this position. Which ones do you think are true?

Things to think about

- Is she the only one to blame?

- Decide what you think the consequences of her actions might be, and who might be the victims.

- What do you think should happen now to help Kim?

The list will give you some of the reasons that Kim might have given for taking the drugs. Do you agree with them? When you've drawn up your points, compare them with others in the class, and answer the questions at the bottom of this page. Try not to think of just the simple answers. The more you think about things that might not be obvious at first, the more likely you are to be working at Levels 5 or 6.

Kim's reasons?

- 'I get bored.'

- 'My friends made me do it.'

- 'I thought this might make my parents listen to me.'

- 'I knew I could just have one go, and stop it after that.'

- 'I was excluded from school, and there was nothing else to do.'

- 'I just wanted to see what it was like.'

- 'Nobody thinks I can do anything at school. Why should anybody care?'

- 'Everyone else seems to be doing it.'

Kim's story

Kim is 15 years old. She attends a large comprehensive school in London and is in the lower groups for most subjects. She gets extra help with her reading. Her parents both work long hours. Her pet dog, Lucy, recently had to be put down.

'I've got lots of friends at school, but most of them are the sort that seem to get into trouble, and that's why I don't bring them home. My parents are quite posh, and they care about what the neighbours think, so I doubt if they would accept them. My older brother is really clever and he's been at university for two years now, and I miss him because he was always really interested in what I did. I remember I won a prize in Year 7, and he was really pleased. The trouble is that my parents keep telling me that I've got to go to university like him, and they won't listen when I tell them that I really want to work in the pet shop near us, because I really love animals. None of the teachers think I could go to university, and one even laughed at me, but my parents are always too busy to listen.

I spend lots of evenings on my own in my room, pretending to do my homework, but it's too hard, and I was getting into trouble at school for not finishing it. Then one day, some of the girls set fire to the waste bin in the science lesson, and I joined in for a laugh. We were all excluded from school for three days, but I didn't dare tell my parents, so I pinched the letter before they could see it, and went out in the mornings like normal. I just hung around in town until home time. I can't say I missed the lessons, but I was frightened at what my dad would do to me when he came back from his business trip and found out. On the second day, this boy who had been thrown out of another school came up to us and offered us some pills, and my friends took them. They gave some to me and I took them as well, but I can't tell you why – not really. I liked the feeling, and since then I've had more because all the others were, but now the boy wants me to pay him money for the pills, and I don't know where I'll get it from.'

- What dangers now face Kim?
- What or who caused Kim's problem?
- What do you think could have been done about it?
- What could be done now to help Kim?

A campaign against drugs

To enable you to plan a small campaign inside the school to make people aware of the dangers of illegal drug use.

This activity will give you practice before the larger activity coming up in Unit 11, and will also give you a chance to assess your own progress.

You will need

- **Paper, for planning and surveys.**
- **Large paper, for posters.**
- **Coloured pens, markers, etc.**
- **A log, to record everything you do.**

For any campaign to be successful, you will have to approach it in stages.

Stage 1

Think hard about what you want to achieve with this campaign.

- Who do you want to inform most – the younger students, or the older ones?
- What do you actually want to tell them, and how are you going to do it?

You might want to give a presentation in assembly, or something that will reach the whole school through posters and leaflets.

- What do you want the overall result of your campaign to be?

Stage 2

Plan your activities carefully. You will need information, and to do research. Your teacher will help you with material. Where will you find your information? This part might take some time, but it's important to be **very accurate**. You can't tell people things that might not be true.

Has your school got an anti-drugs policy? Find out, and see if you agree with it or not. Is there anyone in the group with a story about drugs, perhaps someone they know, that you could use? (It is important to change the name if you do that.)

Could you plan a survey of some other classes to find out what they know about the dangers of drugs? Which teachers might be especially helpful?

Stage 3

Decide how you're going to present the information. How will you design posters, for example, that won't make matters worse? How will you attract the attention of the right age group?

Are you planning to invite anyone in to speak? Your school will have addresses that you can write to, and will show you how to do that for best results. But remember that there is a great deal more to this than just writing a letter. Where will they speak? At what time? Will the students you want to reach be able to be there? How do you check up on all these things first?

Self-assessment

Your teacher will be noting your contribution to the campaign, but this is an activity where you can also assess yourself, because you are keeping a log of everything you do. Use the strands 1, 2 and 3 self-assessment sheets that your teacher will give you, and note any things you have done that might be at Levels 4, 5 or 6. Use a different colour for each level and mark each one off in your log to see how you believe you did.

The long arm of the law

What do you know?

- Have we always had a police force?

- What roles do the police have?

What will you know?

By the end of this unit you will know

- the role and powers of the police

- procedures to be followed when a person is arrested.

Key words: local police authorities, special constables, stop and search, non-arrestable offences, reprimand, charge, bail, custody, final warning, cautions, Youth Offending Team.

Why do we need a police force?

To catch criminals and to keep us safe are two of the reasons we need a police force. That was originally why the police were nicknamed the 'long arm of the law', because most of their job was to catch people committing crimes. Since we first had a national police force in 1856, it has grown to provide much more service than just catching criminals. Look back at all the purposes of having laws in Unit 2 and you'll get a better idea of some of the many things that the police do.

Strictly speaking, there isn't just one police force, but 43 across England and Wales, and all except one – the Metropolitan Police in London – answer to groups of people called **local police authorities**. These are made up of local people, because the idea is that the police are working for all of us as public servants.

All members of the police – and there are over 140 000 of them in England and Wales – have to abide by strict rules laid down by law. The law also gives certain powers to the police.

An early 19th-century policeman, whose job was mainly to catch criminals and to deter others from committing crimes by patrolling in a very recognisable uniform.

More facts about the police

- Over 18 000 people work as **special constables**. Aged between 18 and 50, these volunteers do duties like traffic control, foot patrols and crowd control at football matches.

- Each force has specialist units, such as the Crime Squad, Fraud Squad, Traffic, Horses, Dogs.
- There are other specialist police forces like the London Transport Police.

- There were no women police until 1914, when they were needed because men were fighting in World War I. Now there are about 15 000 women police officers.

❶ How important are the police?

This activity will help you to find out how the police are organised, and some of the many roles they perform.

You will need

- **Coloured pencils.**
- **Large paper for posters.**

You are going to create a display designed to explain to people what police have to do. Ask others in the class what they believe the importance of the police really is, and whether they have ever come into contact with police. If so, in what way, and was their impression a good one?

Your teacher will be able to help you with extra sources of information. You might want to include sections in your display that cover

- the history of the police

- the powers of the police

- the jobs that police do

- why you think police are important in our lives today.

If you have access to the Internet, have a look at two sites – www.police999.com and www.met.police.uk.

The main powers of the police

Note that all these have very strict rules controlled by law. Most police powers were set down in the Police and Criminal Evidence Act 1984.

- **Powers of investigation**
- **Powers of detention and questioning (for a limited time)**
- **Powers of search – persons and property (under certain conditions)**
- **Powers of arrest and charging (according to strict rules)**

Self-assessment

Level 5 students will show that they have a good understanding of the information and can research it carefully, but it's the last part that will bring you more into Level 6 work, particularly if you can include why some people do not seem to like the police much, while others think that they do a very important job. Make sure you find out the whole range of jobs that police are often asked to do. You could again use strands 1, 2 and 3 self-assessment sheets to test your levels for this activity.

Stop and search

Police can arrest anyone they suspect of committing a crime or to be about to commit a crime, and since 1984 have been given much stronger powers to stop and search anyone they have good reason to suspect of carrying banned or stolen articles. One in eight of these searches leads to an arrest.

What do you think of this power? Would the police be unable to do their job without it, or is it against our human rights?

What happens if you are arrested

Every year, police in England and Wales arrest over 2 million people, and about half of these admit their offences. We'll see the procedures that have to be followed if a young person is arrested.

Stage 1

The police may stop and search you if they suspect that you are carrying stolen or banned articles, or that you have committed or are about to commit a crime. Some offences such as speeding are called **non-arrestable**, and the police may just send you a summons to pay a fine or to appear in court on a later date. The police may also arrest you if they ask your name and address and you refuse to give it, or if you insult them or attack them. When they arrest you, they must caution you and tell you your rights as follows.

> 'You do not have to say anything but it may harm your defence if you do not mention when questioned something which you later rely on in court. Anything you say may be given in evidence. Do you understand?'

Read it through carefully. Say exactly what you think it means.

Stage 2

If you are under 17, the police must make sure your parents or a responsible adult described as an 'appropriate adult' is present before you are interviewed. Everyone is entitled to be represented by a solicitor.

Stage 3

The police may interview you, and normally the interview should be taped. If for any reason that is not possible, or if the offence is not very serious, then at least written notes of the interview are essential, and these have to be available afterwards.

Stage 4

If you admit the crime, and the crime is not very serious, then the police have several options. They can either let you go and say there will be no further action, although they might keep a record that you were interviewed. Or they might issue a **reprimand** (a formal notice that you have been in trouble), especially if the offence is not very serious and it's your first time, and this will be kept on record. In some circumstances, the police may decide to **charge** you. In this case they may send you home to wait to see if you will have to go to court, but they might ask for **bail**, when somebody has to put up a certain amount of money to make sure that you will appear in court if called. For a very serious charge, or where you or others might be in danger, they might decide to keep you in **custody** until you can appear in court. The chances are that if it is your first offence, or the crime is not too serious, and you admit to it, they might issue a **final warning**.

Final warnings

These were first introduced in some parts of the country in 1998, and they have replaced the idea of **cautions** for young people. These warnings must be given at a police station by a police officer in the presence of an 'appropriate adult', and may be given if you have not had a warning for two years or have never received one. Nobody can be given more than two warnings, and if you commit a crime after that, you will automatically be taken to court, no matter what the offence. If you receive a warning, your name will be given very quickly to a local **Youth Offending Team**, and their job will be to assess you and probably to decide upon a programme to try to stop you offending again. This might mean some service to the community, or meeting the victim to talk about the effects of the crime on them. The good news is that almost 80 per cent of young offenders who have received a warning do not re-offend within two years.

❷ Kim gets caught

To help you to recognise that young people have rights when they are arrested, but that the police have rights too!

We're going to meet Kim again. She has been arrested for being in possession of illegal substances (drugs) and taken to the police station. Read through this account of what happens, and note down any mistakes that you think were made. Your teacher will go through the answers with you.

Kim's arrest

Stage 1

Kim is stopped and searched by a woman police officer, who finds a small quantity of illegal drugs in Kim's bag. The officer asks for Kim's name and address, but she refuses to give it, and swears at the police officers. Kim is taken to the police station and led straight to an interviewing room, where she is told to sit down in the presence of two policemen.

Stage 2

They tell her that they are going to charge her with possessing illegal substances. Kim admits that she is 15 and tells them that she has never been in trouble before. She tells the police that her parents are away on business. She admits that she has been excluded from school, and that she has kept the letter from her parents, so that they don't know.

Stage 3

The police say that they are not going to tape record the interview, but that they will take notes of what is said. Kim refuses to say anything. The police then tell her that this might count against her if they decide to take matters further. She then says again that she has never been in trouble before.

Stage 4

The police say that they will let Kim go home, but that they will give her a warning, and that if she breaks the law within three years, she will find herself facing charges for this and the new offence.

There are several things that have gone wrong in this account. If this were a real situation the police would have been very careful to follow all the correct procedures. List and discuss the main mistakes that you think have been made. The more you listen to others before you make your points, the more likely you are to be working at least at Level 5. Using all the terms correctly, with accurate comments and details, will probably put you into Level 6. Your teacher will give you the self-assessment sheet for Strand 1 so you can see how you're doing.

What should have happened

Now rewrite the whole incident as another short scene, putting in the corrections and showing what should have happened. You might want to write it like a short play, with others taking some of the roles.

Going to court

- What sort of court are young people most likely to go to if they commit a crime?

- Who decides if you are guilty or innocent in a court?

What will you know?

By the end of this unit you will know

- the way the courts work

- the difference between civil courts and criminal courts

- how the youth courts operate.

You will also learn about sentencing.

Key words: level of proof, burden of proof, jury, electoral register, accused, sentence, appeals, Crown Prosecution Service, magistrate, summary offence, indictable offence, solicitor, barrister, clerk to the justices, stipendiary magistrate.

Civil and criminal courts

The courts are a very important part of our legal system. They aim to make sure that everyone has a fair trial. Remember that there are two different kinds of law – civil and criminal. There are also two different systems of courts to deal with them, and they work in different ways.

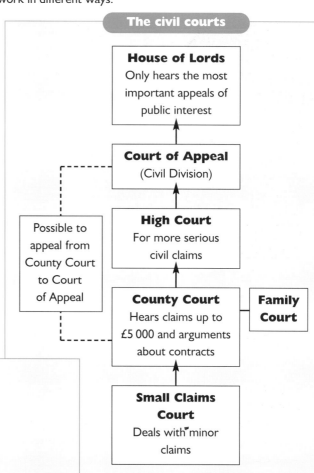

The civil courts

House of Lords
Only hears the most important appeals of public interest

Court of Appeal
(Civil Division)

High Court
For more serious civil claims

Possible to appeal from County Court to Court of Appeal

County Court
Hears claims up to £5 000 and arguments about contracts

Family Court

Small Claims Court
Deals with minor claims

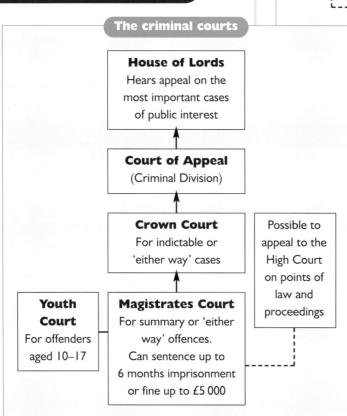

The criminal courts

House of Lords
Hears appeal on the most important cases of public interest

Court of Appeal
(Criminal Division)

Crown Court
For indictable or 'either way' cases

Possible to appeal to the High Court on points of law and proceedings

Youth Court
For offenders aged 10–17

Magistrates Court
For summary or 'either way' offences.
Can sentence up to 6 months imprisonment or fine up to £5 000

The civil courts deal with private law, and here it is only necessary to prove the case on the 'balance of probability'. If I insulted you in public, you might only have to show that I probably did it. In a criminal trial, it would have to be proved 'beyond all reasonable doubt' that a crime was committed. That is known as the **level of proof**. In a criminal court the **burden of proof** falls on the prosecution to prove guilt. Nobody usually has to prove themselves innocent.

Serving on a jury

Another important difference is that in most cases in the Crown Court there is a **jury**. Cases are rarely heard by juries in a civil court. Juries used to be just made up of '12 good men and true', but that would no longer be legal. Today, anybody between the ages of 18 and 70 may be picked from the **electoral register** (the list of names of those who can vote) to serve on a jury in a nearby Crown Court. Their job will be to listen to the evidence and to decide whether the accused is innocent or guilty.

Usually all members of the jury have to agree on a verdict, but in some circumstances the judge will accept a decision of up to 10–2. It is up to the judge to pass **sentence** if the **accused** (the person who has been charged) is found guilty. Serving on a jury is another example of the idea of responsibility that we discussed earlier. There are some people who are not allowed to serve on a jury, including lawyers and police officers, but many of you will find yourself doing this important work at some time in your lives.

This statue stands above the Old Bailey in London, the most famous Crown Court. The scales represent the idea that justice is finely balanced. Can you guess why the figure is blindfolded?

◑ Understanding criminal courts

This activity will help you to understand more about the British system of courts.

The courts

First, copy the diagrams that show the system of criminal and civil courts. We'll be concentrating most on the criminal system, but it's important to understand some of the differences between the two.

How do you think you can find out more details? You can use books from the library or use the Internet. Try www.lcd.gov.uk, which is the site of the Lord Chancellor's Department. This controls the courts in England and Wales. There is more information in the rest of this unit and the next.

In particular, find out what **appeals** are. You can see on the diagrams that it is possible to appeal against a decision if a person is found guilty. That is not easy to do, and usually only happens if there has been something wrong with the way that the case has been handled. Perhaps some important evidence wasn't given, or the case didn't proceed absolutely correctly.

One of the best ways to find out about courts is to visit one, and your teacher may be able to help you arrange this. We'll be looking closely at how a trial is conducted in the next unit.

The **Crown Prosecution Service** (CPS) was set up in 1981 and has a very important role. Before that time, police would often bring prosecutions themselves, but it was felt that the people who brought the charges should not be the same as those who prosecuted in court. Can you see why? The CPS can give advice to the police before they decide to charge someone, and will look at every case to decide whether there is enough evidence to bring the person to court. The CPS will prosecute in cases held in Magistrates Courts and check how cases are going in the Crown Court. Prosecution barristers in the Crown Court will be working to the instructions of the Crown Prosecution Service.

The Magistrates Court

Over 95 per cent of all criminal cases are dealt with in these courts, and without them the system would probably grind to a halt. A **magistrate** (or Justice of the Peace) is usually a respected local citizen who acts as a judge for up to 26 half-days a year. You cannot be a magistrate if you're a serving member of the armed forces, a relative of a magistrate already serving in the same place, or a member of the police force. You have to be at least 27 years old, and will have to retire at 70. Magistrates get expenses, but are usually unpaid.

Magistrates can deal with offences for which the maximum punishment is a fine of up to £5000 or a sentence of up to six months in custody. These offences are called **summary** – they are dealt with in the Magistrates Court itself. These include smaller offences like common assault and many motoring offences. There are others, such as theft, burglary, and drink-driving, that are called 'either way' offences, and these can also be dealt with in the higher court – the Crown Court.

More serious crimes are called **indictable** offences, and these must be tried in the Crown Court. These include serious crimes such as murder, robbery, and rape. At present, everybody who has to appear in court on a criminal charge will first appear at a Magistrates Court to decide what kind of trial he or she should have.

In Britain, we have two main types of lawyer – solicitors and barristers. A **solicitor** can be approached directly by the public, and can speak for you in the lower courts. If the case is held in the Crown Court, you will usually have to be represented by a **barrister**, who is appointed by the solicitor on your behalf. There are a few solicitors who are now allowed to represent you in the Crown Court. A barrister is usually an expert in particular kinds of law.

❷ ▶ Some questions to think about

These questions are designed to get you thinking about the role of the magistrates in our system of courts.

Think about the information you have read and then read the information below and answer the questions that follow.

Magistrate or jury?

There are nearly two million people dealt with by magistrates every year. Of these just under half a million are 'either way' cases and just under 1.5 million are summary. Of the 'either way' cases, about 28 per cent want to go to the Crown Court. Over 90 per cent of those accused of summary offences plead guilty, compared with about 60 per cent of those who appear in Crown Court.

Most magistrates are unpaid and receive little training in the law. They usually sit in threes, and are helped by a trained lawyer while conducting the case. He or she is the **Clerk to the Justices**. There are a few paid magistrates in the larger cities, called **stipendiary** magistrates.

1. What does it mean when it says that 1.5 million cases are summary?

2. Why do you think that 28 per cent of 'either way' cases want to go before a jury in Crown Court?

3. Why do you think that only 60 per cent of those facing charges in the Crown Court plead guilty?

4. Most criminal cases are dealt with by magistrates. Magistrates are not trained lawyers, and because there's no jury, they have to decide themselves whether a person is innocent or guilty. What do you think would happen if we got rid of all the magistrates?

How your work will be assessed

After you have discussed these questions, your teacher will read your answers, but the following might help you when you are thinking about what to say.

Level 4

You show that you understand how the Magistrates Court works and some of the differences between the Magistrates Court and the Crown Court.

Level 5

You show that you have found out more information from other sources, and are expressing some opinions about the importance of the magistrates.

Level 6

You show that you have listened to the opinions of others and are arguing your case using words that you didn't use before.

Before you hand in your work, go through your answers and mark off any parts that you think might fit into the levels outlined above. Use a code or a different colour to show each level.

The Youth Courts

One of the most important roles of the Magistrates Court is to act as a Youth Court. Youth Courts were introduced in 1992 to replace the older system of juvenile courts that had been operating for nearly a century. They are magistrates courts, but they look different, and the cases are heard in a different way. Anybody between the ages of 10 and 17 accused of a crime should appear in a Youth Court, unless they are over 14 and charged with a 'grave crime' like indecent assault or dangerous driving, or worse. A young person might also appear in an adult court if he or she is charged jointly with a person over 18.

In a Youth Court, the magistrates are specially trained to deal with young people, and must not be over 65 years old. At least one magistrate on each case should be a woman. Often, the furniture will be rearranged so that everybody sits at the same level, and lawyers will wear ordinary clothes, as will the police. The accused will be allowed to sit between his or her parents, and the atmosphere is deliberately made to feel less frightening. There is usually a lot more discussion in a Youth Court, and the idea is to involve the young person so that he or she understands what has happened and the consequences of the crime.

Youth Justice Board News

Sentencing

One of the important roles of a judge is to pass sentence if the defendant is found or pleads guilty. Could you do that in a way that is absolutely fair, without letting your personal feelings get in the way? A magistrate in a Youth Court now has a very wide range of sentences that he or she can pass. First, let's think about why we sentence people after they've committed a crime.

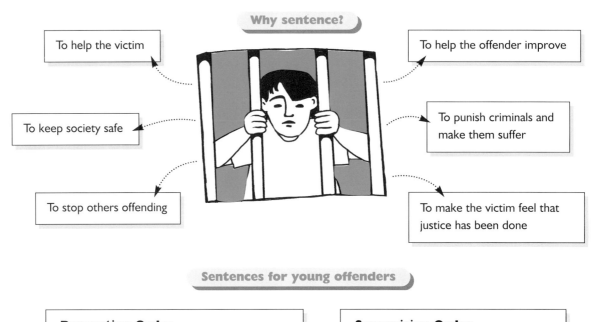

Why sentence?

To help the victim

To keep society safe

To stop others offending

To help the offender improve

To punish criminals and make them suffer

To make the victim feel that justice has been done

Sentences for young offenders

Reparation Order
To try to put things right. It may mean putting damage right or apologising to the victim.

Supervision Order
Often a three-month action plan supervised by a probation officer, social worker or Youth Offending Team.

Referral Order
Standard for first-time offenders. Young people are referred to a Youth Offending Panel if they plead guilty. They are assessed and perhaps given training and made to put things right.

Compensation Order
Usually up to £1 000 for a Youth Court.

Detention and Training Order
For 15- to 17-year-olds. Half the time can be spent in custody and half in the community under supervision. Young offenders can be sentenced like this for offences that could mean prison if they were older.

Secure Training Centres
For persistent offenders aged 12 to 14 and others.

Parenting Order
Compulsory for parents of all young offenders of up to 16, usually to make parents take responsibility. Parents will be fined if the young person offends again within a year. Parenting Orders can last three years.

Attendance Order
For young offenders to report to a local centre for instruction up to three hours a day.

③ The purpose of sentencing

This activity will make you think about how difficult it is to pass the right sentence in a range of different circumstances.

A judge in a Crown Court wears a wig and robes.

What to do

Copy out the reasons given under 'Why sentence?' on page 28. Which of these reasons do you think is the most important? Discuss these in small groups, and listen to the reasons why some might disagree with your choice.

Should we think most about stopping criminals repeating their acts, or should we make it up to the victims by treating the criminals harshly? If we do try to stop them repeating their crimes, should we do that by frightening them, or by helping them to understand that what they are doing is wrong for others? Write down your conclusions before you go on to the next part.

Now look at the second diagram, about sentences for young offenders. Take each of the possible sentences and say what you think is its main purpose. Is it to punish the criminal, to help the victim, to help the criminal, or more than one of these? Write each one down in the correct column of a chart like this.

Punishment	To help the victim	To help the criminal	More than one purpose

Two cases

Read the following examples, and decide what sentence you would impose if you were the magistrate. Remember to think carefully about all the possible consequences, but also that you are there to make sure that justice is done. You won't find it as easy as you think.

Remember, the more reasons you give for your answers, the higher level you will achieve.

Case A

Manjit has been found guilty of helping her friends steal an old lady's handbag. She is 14. It is her first offence. She has three very young brothers and sisters that she helps her sick mother look after. She told the court that she didn't care if they 'sent her away' because she was fed up with her hard life at home, and would only do it again to make her life less boring.

Case B

Chris is 12, and he attacked a boy outside school, causing serious injuries to the boy's face that needed stitches. He pleaded guilty in the court, but said that he was only protecting his young brother, Alan, who is 8 years old. The boy had seen Chris and Alan setting fire to some rubbish in the park, and was about to tell the police. Chris's parents were in court, and admit that they cannot keep the boys in at night. Chris has had a final warning six months before for fighting, and Alan has been brought home several times by the police for causing trouble late at night. Their parents plead with the magistrate to give the boys another chance, saying that they are very well behaved at home, and care about their family a great deal.

Martin's trial

What do you know?

- What happens in a trial?
- What sort of things are you not allowed to say in a trial?

What will you know?

By the end of this unit you will understand the role of the

- magistrates
- prosecuting and defence lawyers
- clerk to the justices
- court usher.

You will also know what is meant by rules of evidence.

People in the court

We are going to conduct a trial in the Youth Court. The first thing to decide is what part you're going to play. For this trial, we're going to need the following.

- **Three magistrates** – whose role it is to preside over the case, to decide a verdict and to pass sentence if Martin (the accused) is found guilty.

- **Lawyers** – one for the prosecution case, and one to defend Martin.

- **Witnesses** – two for the prosecution and two for the defence, including Martin.

- **Court officers** – a clerk and an usher. If necessary, one person could take both these roles.

- **Reporters** – to write about the trial, and to sum up the main decisions.

('R.' stands for *Regina*, meaning the Queen. That is because the Crown Prosecution Service prosecutes on behalf of the monarchy, representing the people.)

❶ R. vs Martin Jones

By carrying out this trial, you will learn more about how justice works, and some of the difficulties faced by those whose job it is to uphold the law.

Some important rules

Remember that this is a criminal court, and you will have to believe that Martin is guilty beyond reasonable doubt if he is to be convicted and sentenced. You will need to listen very carefully to the evidence. It's important not to make up new evidence from your own imagination, but you can get into character and say what would be in keeping with the part you are playing.

The magistrates

If you're feeling full of wisdom, you might want to take the part of the magistrates, whose job it is to decide whether Martin is guilty, and to pass sentence. Remember the options that are open to you, and the purposes of sentencing – if you get the chance, of course. Three of you will be deciding whether Martin is guilty or not.

The lawyers

The lawyers for the defence and the prosecution have to follow strict rules. Look at the diagram, which shows the order that the trial must take.

There are rules about the type of questions you are allowed to ask. You mustn't ask **leading questions** like 'You don't like him much, do you?' Instead, you should say 'Tell the court what you think about him.' Notice also that when you're **cross-examining** (questioning a witness) you're not allowed to bring in any new evidence, but must simply try to correct any bad impression created during the preceding examination. Your witnesses, for example, may have been made to look as if they aren't honest. You will have to ask questions that try to correct that.

The lawyers should not rehearse everything beforehand. You'll need to listen to the witnesses before you can decide what questions you'll ask. Be sure to take plenty of notes. Go for weaknesses in the evidence or where the witness may have contradicted him or herself. Remember that the defence lawyer does not have to prove that Martin is innocent. The prosecution lawyer has to prove him guilty beyond a reasonable doubt. When you've finished, you say 'That is the case for the prosecution/defence.'

The order of events in a criminal trial

1. Prosecution opening speech describing the crime

2. Prosecution witness examined by the prosecution (after they have been sworn in by the Usher)

3. Defence cross-examines witness (2 and 3 happen for each prosecution witness)

4. Defence witness examined by the defence

5. Prosecution cross-examines defence witness (Note that defence can re-examine each witness if stage 5 has caused problems for their case)

6. Closing speech of prosecution

7. Closing speech of defence

8. Clerk to the Justices advises magistrates on the law

9. Magistrates retire and consider verdict

10. Magistrates announce verdict, explaining to the defendant why they have come to their decision

11. If guilty, defendant is sentenced

The witnesses

Each witness has a basic set of notes, and you should study these carefully. You're allowed to get into character, and that will make a difference to how the magistrates will judge the statement you make. Try not to make things up, but it is perfectly alright to say things that fit in with your notes and the background of the character. Don't just read out the whole statement, but wait until you are asked questions. Remember not to put forward opinions – they aren't allowed.

The clerk and the usher

These are important roles in keeping the court working properly. The **clerk** sits at the front and will inform the magistrates of the case and with which crime Martin is charged. He or she will also advise the magistrates on points of law at the end of the case, and read out any written statements. The **usher's** role is to call the witnesses and make them take the oath before they are questioned – 'I do solemnly, sincerely and truly declare and affirm that the evidence I shall give shall be the truth, the whole truth, and nothing but the truth.'

The reporters

This could be the rest of the class and your role will be to write an accurate report of the trial, explaining what happened stage by stage, and explaining the verdict and the sentence, if that happens. You will need to pay attention to the character of the witnesses and the way the questions are being answered. Do they seem nervous and unsure? The object is to write clearly and to make it interesting. You might also want to comment on the verdict.

The facts

The first thing to do is to read the facts and notes that will accompany this case. After that, when everyone has their roles, act out the trial following the order of events on page 31.

Martin's statement

'I'm 16 years old, and a very hard-working student at the local grammar school. I am expected to get all my GCSEs and have been working very hard towards them. My parents would like me to go to university like my sister, and I would like to become a doctor. On the morning of May 17th, I was in town taking a break from my revision when I heard a burglar alarm going off in a nearby shop. As I went to see what was happening, a boy collided with me. He was one of my classmates – Joe Turner – who handed me a watch and told me to put it into my pocket. I did so, and Joe told me that he had bought it for his father, but that another boy was trying to steal it from him. I asked him about the alarm, and he told me that when the boy chased him, the shop assistant had thought they were stealing the watch and pressed the alarm button. Joe told me that he was just about to pay for the watch when this happened. The trouble was that no one would believe him now, but he promised to send the watch back to the shop as soon as he got home. He asked me to take it home for him and that he would collect it later. Before I could say anything, he had run off and two policemen caught hold of me. They searched me and found the watch. I was later charged with theft because they said Joe told them that I was involved in the whole thing, and Joe said I told him to steal it for me. I don't know why he said that.'

The written statement of the arresting officer – to be read out by the clerk at the beginning of the trial, before the prosecution's opening speech

'I was called to the shop at 3.15 pm on May 17th and was directed by the shop assistant to the defendant (Martin), who was standing some 50 metres from the entrance and was turning to leave. The assistant explained to me that she had seen the defendant take possession of the said item – a watch – and I explained to him that I had reason to believe that he was in possession of stolen goods. He was duly searched, and the stolen property was discovered in his pocket. When questioned in the presence of his parents at 5.00 pm he told us that the watch had been given to him by a friend – Joseph Turner. Mr Turner was later questioned and told us in a statement that the defendant had forced him into carrying out the theft and that he would have split the proceeds of the sale with him. This was later corroborated (agreed on) by Mr Turner's father, who had witnessed the conversation in their house the previous night. Joseph Turner knew nothing of any other persons trying to take the watch from them in the shop. Because of special circumstances, Joseph Turner is currently the subject of separate enquiries for other offences, and has been badly injured in a road accident. He is recovering in St Mary's Hospital but still in some discomfort, and hence cannot appear in this court.'

Prosecution witnesses

1 Mary Campbell – shop assistant, aged 59 years

'I was serving several customers, when this boy came up to the counter and grabbed the watch. Before I could stop him, he had run out of the shop. I'd just come back to work after an operation on my eyes, so I couldn't chase him. I pressed the alarm and went to the door. Two policemen were driving past and I stopped them. I saw the boy who had been in the shop about 50 metres away, and he looked a troublemaker. He was laughing and chatting with the defendant, and I saw him hand over the watch and run off. Then two policemen came and stopped the defendant and searched him. Then they put him in the car and came back to question me. I swear the defendant was laughing at me as he sat in the back of the police car.'

2 Archie Turner (the other boy's father) – unemployed, aged 62 years

'I was dozing in my chair, half-watching the TV. I'd been out for a few drinks and felt tired. My son and the defendant were sitting in the kitchen and the door was slightly open. I heard raised voices and somebody said "You'd better do this", or something like that, "because I need that present for my dad." I couldn't hear too much more, but I know that somebody said something like "It's only a watch. You'd be wise to do it." After he had gone, my boy looked very scared, but he wouldn't talk to me about it. That's not the first time he's been shouted at by Martin. Ideas above his station if you ask me. I swear worrying about this is what made him have that accident.'

Witnesses for the defence

1 The first witness called by the defence is Martin himself

2 Sheila Gush – Martin's headteacher

'I can honestly say that Martin is usually very well behaved in school. His parents are very supportive and have promised a very generous contribution to the school library if Martin does well in his GCSEs. I can't recall his teachers telling me that Martin was ever in trouble – except that time when he was punished for bullying in Year 9, but boys will be boys and as far as I know he hasn't done that since. I'm told that Martin is working far too hard. He's been off school lately, and I don't know about his health. He seems under stress, but I'm sure he'll cope with the exams. After all, he comes from a very good family and has never been in trouble with the police. His parents make sure he has everything he wants.'

One final point. The law says that **theft** means to take somebody else's property dishonestly with the intention of **permanently** depriving the owner of it. The fact that Martin was not actually in the shop may not be important if there is a suggestion that the whole thing was his idea. If proven, that would make him as guilty as the other boy.

The prosecution has to prove that the watch was taken dishonestly, and not by accident, and that there was no intention of giving it back.

Enjoy the trial.

Changing the law – let's debate!

What do you know?

- Do laws always have to stay the same?

- Can you think of any laws that you believe should be changed?

What will you know?

By the end of this unit you will know

- how to take part in a debate

- how to decide whether we should make the law stronger on particular matters.

Should the law be made stricter to protect animals?

Bear baiting was once accepted but is now illegal.

Most people think that in Britain we're kind to animals, and compared with some countries we may be right. We have many laws that are designed to protect animals, and many cruel practices like cock fighting and bear baiting were stopped long ago.

However, many people believe that some laws aren't strict enough. Take battery farming, for example. European law will make sure that from 2012, hens are not bred in small cages, but in the meantime many say that animals will continue to suffer. Laws like the Protection of Animals Act 1911 try to ensure that conditions are as good as possible, but the fine for causing unnecessary suffering is only £5 000 or up to six months in prison. Considering that we consume over 800 million chickens every year, it would be very difficult to make sure that every bird was well treated.

And what about the use of animals for other purposes, such as circuses, zoos and sport? Laws try to control the way these animals are treated, but do we have any right at all to use animals in this way? Should the law ban these activities altogether?

Which activities, if any, should be banned?

Experiments on animals

We're going to concentrate on the subject of using animals in scientific experiments. The law says that it is not a crime to do this if it advances our knowledge of science, helps us prevent or treat disease, or helps us to understand how animals, plants or humans function. Every year, about three million experiments involving animals take place in Britain. Most of them use rats and mice, but several thousand each year involve the use of larger animals such as dogs and cats. Laws attempt to control the use of these animals and try to stop unnecessary suffering. But many still argue that we should not be carrying out experiments like this at all, whatever the reason.

❶ 'We believe that the use of any animal in an experiment should be made a criminal offence'

By taking part in a debate on the motion (subject) above, you will work out what you believe about this aspect of the law and practise arguing your case to an audience.

What other people say

Read through these extracts carefully. They show some arguments on both sides. You could use them whether you are presenting one of the cases or speaking from the audience.

❶ The fundamental problem of animal-based research is called 'species differences'. Every species responds differently to various substances, and this causes problems when researchers apply results from animal tests to people. Animals are not like us, they react differently to products, they suffer from different diseases, and artificial disease created in the laboratory is not the same as spontaneous disease suffered by people in the real world. A further complication of animal tests is that the distress caused to the animals by being caged in a laboratory can also affect the outcome of the experiment. We are opposed to violence to animals and to humans.

(The National Anti-Vivisection Society)

❷ 'MI5 has been called in by the Government to help track down animal rights extremists behind an escalation [rapid increase] of urban terrorism. In the latest attack, a nail-filled letter bomb exploded in a North Wales fish and chip shop yesterday. The owner, Jonathan Davies, a country sports enthusiast, was uninjured when a shower of nails hit the floor of the busy shop.'

(*Daily Telegraph*, 2001)

❸ 'Animal research is essential to help scientists evaluate the effectiveness of new medicines... The biological similarities between ourselves and other animals are enormous... There are, of course, species differences between ourselves and other animals but compared to the similarities, the differences are minor.'

(The Association of the British Pharmaceutical Industry)

❹ 'Research involving animals has to be designed so that any distress or suffering involved is kept to a minimum. For example, if the experiment would hurt the animal, an anaesthetic or painkiller would normally be given.'

(Research Defence Society)

Notice that extract 2 isn't strictly about animal experimentation. Why do you think it has been included, and how could you use it in this debate?

Some arguments for and against

To help you, here are some of the main arguments put forward on both sides. Consider them all and try to add at least one more for each side.

No. The law should not be changed.

- If we didn't test treatments on animals we would have to test them on humans, and that's obviously wrong.

- The law already has controls over how experiments are carried out.

- Many vital discoveries in science and medicine that have alleviated human suffering have only happened with the help of animal experimentation.

- Animals themselves will benefit from some of the research.

- Humans should always come first. Animals don't have rights in the same way that humans do.

Yes. The law should be changed.

- Instead of experimenting on animals, we should be working to make people live more healthily to prevent diseases happening.

- Experiments don't have to be done on animals. It doesn't actually tell us that much about what the effect would be on humans.

- The maximum fine for cruelty to animals is £5 000. That isn't enough.

- We should be willing to be ill rather than hurt animals like this.

- The law is too vague. All it stops is 'unnecessary suffering'. What does that really mean?

The rules of debate

You'll probably want to find out more about the subject. When you're ready to start the debate, you'll have to follow some important rules to keep the debate running smoothly. A good debate needs the following people.

- A chairperson.

- One or two speakers either side. The first speaker is called the **proposer**, and the second is called the **seconder**. One side defends the motion (the statement) and the other speaks against it.

- An audience.

The debate, controlled by the chairperson, carries on in the following order.

- The chairperson introduces the subject and explains the rules.

- The first speaker argues **against** the motion (about five minutes).

- The first speaker on the other side argues **for** the motion (about five minutes).

- The seconder then argues against the motion, picking up some of the points that have just been made (about five minutes).

- The second speaker for the motion counteracts the argument just made (about five minutes).

- The chairperson throws it open to the audience, taking questions one at a time. Here, the audience can either just make their points, or challenge one of the speakers with a question.

- A speaker on each side sums up, starting with speakers against the motion. Here, each speaker should try to make a clear summary of why the audience should vote with him or her.

- The audience votes. The motion is either '**carried**' (agreed with) or '**rejected**' (disagreed with).

Remember, this is a debate about the law, so keep to the subject. Too many facts and figures can make the audience bored. Always listen respectfully when someone makes a point, and never speak unless the chairperson allows you to. Never lose your temper or be rude to the other side, however much you disagree with the argument. When you state your points, make them clear and brief.

If you're in the audience, you should use an audience sheet like the one on page 37, and hand it in to your teacher at the end.

National Anti-Vivisection Society

A macaque monkey undergoing brain experiments at the Institute of Neurology, London.

Audience sheet

Copy the table below and fill it in as you listen to the debate, then hand it in to your teacher.

'We believe that the use of any animal in an experiment should be made a criminal offence'	
Main arguments presented	
For	Against

Points I would like to raise

....

....

....

How your work will be assessed

Your teacher will assess you not only for the contribution you make, but also for the way you've grasped the points put forward by each side. Listening carefully to other people and understanding their arguments means that you'll be working at Level 5, and persuading other people might take you to Level 6.

Enjoy the debate!

Alternative motions

Here are some other subjects you might like to try.

- 'We should be allowed to marry at 16, even without our parents' permission.'

- 'Prisons don't serve any purpose. They just make criminals worse.'

- 'We can leave school at 16. We should also be allowed to drink alcohol in pubs.'

Talking about crime

- Do you think crime is increasing?
- How does the media influence our perceptions of crime?

- How fear of crime is increased by many factors.
- How the media can influence our perceptions of crime and criminals.

Fear of crime

Look at some of these headlines. We see headlines like these a lot in our newspapers, and they may have helped to shape our ideas, especially when it comes to young people. Have you ever found that many people – older people especially – get very suspicious if they see a large group of youths loitering in a shopping centre, or talking on the corner of a street? One of the reasons for this is fear of crime, and false ideas that all young people in groups must be up to no good. Sometimes, of course, that's true, but it isn't always. Look at the boxes below. They show some of the main reasons why there is this fear of crime today.

ONE PERSON CRIME WAVE!

Bring back flogging!

Boys bragged of killing

Cage the yobs!

What's wrong with young people today?

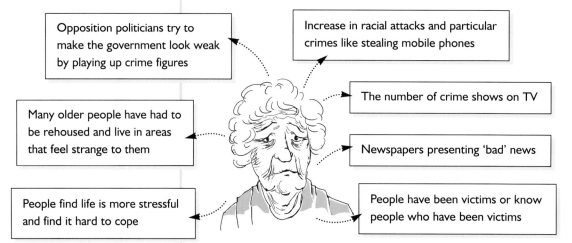

Opposition politicians try to make the government look weak by playing up crime figures

Increase in racial attacks and particular crimes like stealing mobile phones

Many older people have had to be rehoused and live in areas that feel strange to them

The number of crime shows on TV

Newspapers presenting 'bad' news

People find life is more stressful and find it hard to cope

People have been victims or know people who have been victims

Which of these do you think are the most common reasons?

A recent survey showed that it wasn't just old people who feared crime. Some 48 per cent of 17- to 24-year-olds were frightened of crime involving their cars. Another survey showed that 27 per cent of females in that age group were worried about burglary, 37 per cent about rape, and 33 per cent about general physical attack.

More people than ever are having extra locks and alarms fitted to their houses. The supply and fitting of these increased from 52 per cent in 1992 to 75 per cent in 2000. At the same time the prison population in England and Wales has increased dramatically from 45 000 in 1971 to over 72 000 today. All this is giving people the impression that crime is on the increase, that there is more need to be frightened of crime today.

Yet the overall crime rate is going down

In fact, the overall crime figures are going down, as they are in most European countries. Here are some of the possible reasons.

- More people are in work now, and therefore do not become involved in crime.

- More people can afford to buy things that previously they might have stolen.

- Cars and houses are better protected.

- Governments have put a lot of effort into getting certain kinds of crime down.

- People don't walk around with so much cash. They prefer to use credit cards.

Can you think of any more reasons?

One of the reasons why people increasingly fear crime is the way that it's often reported in the newspapers. There is no doubt that crime is still a huge problem, and that in some areas it might be getting worse. But perhaps the fact that there are so many crime shows on television and that the news seems to be full of crime reports makes us believe that life is always like that. In the next unit we'll see how we might do something to show that young people do care about such things. What we're going to do here is to see how we might want to change a newspaper report to show a rather different story to the one that's been reported.

A teenage 'crime wave'?

In this activity you will rewrite a newspaper report to bring out some of the reasons why the story really happened and make people understand it better.

What to do

First read this case study, and see what impression you get.

John is 14 years old. He has 30 convictions for theft, assault and robbery. He lives in a small town where there is not much to do in the evenings for the young people of the area. His mother died when he was two years old, and his father is an unemployed alcoholic who has had to look after four children on his own.

John was truanting from school when he was seven years old, and his father did very little to get him back to school. John would listen to his father shouting at the Educational Welfare Officer on the doorstep when they tried to get him back to school, and several times his father was fined for not making sure John received a proper education. John was put into care at the age of nine.

John was not a very tall boy for his age, and others in the care home made fun of him because of his lack of height. At night he would slip out and join up with a gang of older boys. Soon he began to steal bikes, and at the age of 10 joined them in stealing a car.

By the age of 11 he was taking cannabis, and the gang was well known in the area. The police tended to leave the gang alone if they were not actually seen to be committing a crime, and John and his gang soon learned how to avoid them. They would break into houses but neighbours did not complain very often, because they were afraid that they might get bricks thrown through their windows.

John appeared in court many times from the age of 10 to 14, but it was always felt that it would harm him more to send him to a closed centre. A local newspaper named him, and referred to him as a 'one-boy crime wave'. The rest of his gang looked up to him more after that, and he soon became their leader.

When John was 14, the police arrested him again when he was a passenger in a stolen car. He got another warning but was arrested a month later for stabbing a boy in the leg who called him 'shortie'. Two months ago he appeared in the local youth court and was finally sentenced to a term of six months in a secure centre. There he has met Dan, a convicted drugs dealer who is 16 years old.

39

Reporting the case

No one doubts that John deserves to be arrested and that his crimes had to stop. What follows is the newspaper report of John's case as it might have appeared in the local paper. Read it through carefully, and make notes on all the things you think it

should have included to give a fairer picture. Note also the things it **should not** have said if it is to give a true picture of youth problems and of youth crime. Look at the kinds of words it is using.

TEENAGE THUG CAGED AT LAST!

Justice at last caught up with a young hooligan when he was sentenced to six months' detention for terrorising local people. His seven-year reign of terror was ended when police arrested him for viciously attacking another youth. The boy, who is 14 years old, had systematically terrified locals over a long period of time, attacking people, throwing bricks at their property, and generally defying the law. This newspaper hopes that it will be the first step in ridding our area of the young people who swarm here at night, causing harm to innocent local people. One resident, who did not want to be named, said last night 'Good riddance. It's time that this area was cleaned up. Gangs of youths have made our lives a misery.' This newspaper will certainly be supporting any campaign to rid our streets of young villains who should be doing something more honest like going to school. We would also argue that compulsory national service in the armed forces should be brought back to teach young people discipline.

There is some truth in this report, but to be a useful picture that does not increase people's fear of crime unnecessarily it could have been written in a different way. Your task is to decide how. Remember that you will need to report the story honestly, but try to put something more positive into it. For example, there is no mention of John's poor family life – and what about all the young people in the area who cause no harm?

How your work will be assessed

When you've finished, your teacher will assess the work. Good accurate reporting of the facts of John's case will gain you at least Level 4, and more comments about some of the reasons why John's life developed as it did will earn you marks at Level 5. In addition, a report that tries to lessen people's fear of crime and tries to correct some of the false impressions people might have of young people in general will probably be judged at Level 6.

Making a difference

What do you know?

Throughout this book, we've covered many of the basic facts about crime and law. We've looked at some of the reasons why crimes happen, and learned some of the ways we try to deal with them. We've also examined briefly the fear of crime in some sections of society.

What will you know?

This final unit will give you a chance to think about some ways in which you can make a contribution to helping with the problems caused by crime.

Key words: deterrent, curfew.

Crime prevention

Unit 10 showed us that often people are more worried about becoming victims of crime than they need to be, and see all young people in the same way, as potential young offenders. Can we do anything about that? There are two main ways that we can try to prevent crimes happening. We can punish people to put others off, and we can try to educate more people into understanding why crimes might be committed in the first place. That leads on to trying to change those conditions. The first is called a **deterrent**, to frighten criminals and stop them re-offending, and to stop others copying them. Many would say that the second way is more positive, and tries to show people that they can make something of themselves, and that they don't need to turn to crime to be successful. It is much harder to do than the first way.

Look at these two lists, and see which one you think would produce the better results.

Different approaches to crime prevention

I Using deterrents

- Put more emphasis on sentences that put people in prison.

- Make prison sentences longer.

- Make prison life harsher.

- Issue on-the-spot fines for offenders caught by the police.

- Make sure all criminals are punished after a final warning, whatever their crime.

- Speed up the whole process from arrest to sentence.

- Impose more child **curfews** (stopping children being out after a certain time).

- Fine parents more.

Different approaches to crime prevention

2 Some alternatives to deterrents

- Give criminals the chance to do more work for the community.

- Raise educational standards to fight boredom and truancy in schools.

- Find out more about why people commit crimes and try to change those situations.

- Try to spot possible young criminals early.

- Arrange for criminals to talk to the victims to find out the effects of their crimes.

- Make sure that more criminals get proper training so that they can get jobs.

- Provide more activities for young people during the school holidays to stop them getting bored.

You could probably think of more for each list. People argue about which approach is best, and sometimes the best way may be to take ideas from both lists, because a lot will depend on who the criminals are, why they have offended, and the kinds of crimes they have committed. One thing is certain – there is no easy answer to the problem of crime.

What we can do is to try to help as many people as possible get involved in some of the things you have thought about as you've gone through this book. That's why we're going to spend some time thinking about a school project that might contribute to this. We'll call it **crime awareness**.

 # A school crime awareness project

In this activity you will use the ideas you have gained from this book to help spread more understanding of crime and the problems associated with crime.

Your contribution to this will depend on what you're good at, and which subjects you found most interesting. What follows are some suggestions as to what you might include with your teacher's help, and the help of the rest of your class.

The subjects

Use the boxes on page 43 to remind yourself of the main topics that we might want to make people aware of, and suggest some ways in which we might be able to present them. Remember that you've already done a lot of this work. You might, however, want to change the appearance of some of it for display purposes.

Why do we have law, and where does law come from?

- Posters showing rights and responsibilities and how Parliament makes law.

- Acting out small plays to show what life might be like without laws.

- Writing for display in the classroom or corridors about different kinds of law.

- Writing poems to show the importance of rights to us all.

What crimes are

- Research about different kinds of crime.

- Use a TV magazine to draw up a list of all the main crime programmes that are on the television. What do they all have in common? How many are actually about crime in Britain, and how many about crime in other countries like America?

Drugs

- You could use a lot of the work that you did earlier for Unit 5.

- Try to find out if the law has changed for drugs like cannabis.

- Why not consider a short play on the subject for an assembly?

- This might be a good opportunity to invite in a guest speaker. We'll say more on how to do that on page 44.

The work of the police

- Your local police station will have someone who would be pleased to come in to speak to the school, as long as they get enough notice. That's why it's important to plan early.

- Use your work from Unit 6 to prepare posters and displays about the work of the police.

The courts

- This subject is a good opportunity to make more posters to show what the courts are and how they are organised.

- What about staging the trial you did in Unit 8 for other students to watch?

- Your teacher may be able to help you to get a magistrate into school to talk to a class or assembly about their work.

- If you have ever visited a court, write about the experience. Write a report about a court programme on television.

Views on youth crime

- Ask your teacher or parents to help you collect any articles in the newspapers that deal with young offenders, and see how they are written. You could make a large display of these and add your own comments about them.

- Just as important, have a section in your crime awareness project to discuss what we can do about crime, and what can be done to make people less frightened of it. After all, the proportion of people who actually commit crimes is very small compared with the whole population.

- Perhaps you could stage another debate on a crime topic. Look back at Unit 10 to remind you about that.

- School assemblies are also an excellent chance to present these points, perhaps in the form of a short play.

Putting it together

Once you've decided which areas you are going to deal with, you need to think about the difficult business of putting it all together so that it fits in with what everybody wants. You'll have to discuss this with others and your teacher. A possible crime awareness project might end up as a whole day, and might go something like this.

1. Introduction by a guest speaker, perhaps a representative of the police, or a magistrate. This might take place in assembly, depending on the order of your school day. Your teacher will need to help you with these arrangements.

2. A mock trial, perhaps held for your whole year group, or others. It will be important for someone to explain to the audience beforehand what is happening so that it is easier to understand.

3. The chance for all students to look at the displays during breaks and lunchtimes.

4. A talk, perhaps on drug awareness, by a representative of the police, or a representative from the prison service to talk about recent changes in prisons.

5. A final session about crime prevention. For this it might be possible for everybody who has taken part to join in. Local senior citizens might be invited to contribute, as they will have important ideas about the subject, and will be able to explain what aspects of crime they fear most. Perhaps some will have their own experience as victims of crime. Be sure that someone invites the local paper. After all, the day is all about showing that young people do care about preventing crime, and the more people that hear of your project the better.

What exactly you do will depend on what is possible within your school, but the secret is to start early. Your teacher will tell you what might be possible, and when the best time might be, but the main work will be done by you and your class. Remember the following points.

- Do the parts that you can do best, and spread the work around as much as possible. The whole project will look much better if a lot of people are involved. Draw up a chart like this one, and pin it to the wall so that everyone knows exactly what his or her jobs are. Planning carefully at this early stage is vital.

MAKING A DIFFERENCE

A crime awareness project by the students of
.... School, Class ....

Subject	Activities to be included	Done by [date] Person responsible

- With your teacher, find out at an early stage which day or days would be best for the project, and make sure everybody understands the deadline for the work to be finished.

- Your teacher may prefer to write to people to invite them to speak, but if that is one of your jobs, make sure you remember that outside speakers are very busy people and will need to know exactly what is required of them. A letter for a speaker may go something like the one on the right.

Dear Sir/Madam

[your teacher may know a name to write to]

Crime awareness project at _____
[school] on _____ [date]

Our class is preparing an important crime awareness day to be held at this school on _____. We plan to invite a number of people who are involved in the subject locally, and would be delighted if you could provide a representative to speak to a group of students in Year _____ on the subject of _____.
We would ask that the talk last about ____ minutes, and would be timed to begin at _____ am/pm. We all believe that the day will be an important one, and would therefore be very pleased if someone from your organisation would be able to come. If you would like to participate, please let us know if you will require any special equipment, such as an overhead projector.

We look forward to hearing from you.

Yours sincerely

[Your name]

Finally, remember on the day itself that someone should meet the speaker as they arrive. Have a programme of the day's events ready to give to them so that they can see exactly where they fit in. Be sure to write to them afterwards, thanking them for their contribution. That way, they'll want to come again.

Your project may not end up as large as this suggestion – or it may even spread into two days! Whatever size it is, it will be an important contribution to informing others of the work you have done from this book.

The important thing is to enjoy it. Good luck with the project!

How your work will be assessed

All your work in this unit will be assessed, and there is plenty of opportunity for you to do well. Strand 3 assessments are about contributing to activities, and you will certainly be doing that, whatever your skills. Keep a log of all the things you do towards the project, and you can use the self-assessment sheets to mark off what you have done at different levels.

Multiple choice test

What level have you reached?

Much of the work that you've done throughout this book has been marked against Levels 4, 5 and 6. Here are 15 multiple choice questions so you can check to see how well you know the subjects that you've looked at.

Before you do the test

Read through all the previous work that you've completed. Don't worry if you haven't done them all – you don't need to get every question correct to be awarded a certain level, and some of the questions are testing your skill at using information rather than your ability to remember lots of detail.

Look back at the 'What do you know?' and 'What will you know?' sections that appear throughout the units. These provide a very good revision tool.

Instructions for completing the test

Each question has three answers but only **one** of the answers is correct.

On a separate piece of paper write down the numbers 1–15 in a list and by the side of each number write down what you think is the correct answer for the question. If you think the correct answer for question 1 is (c) then write 1.c, and so on.

After the test

Your teacher has an answer sheet from the Teacher's Guide to this series. He or she will go through the correct answers with you. If you get three out of five questions right in a particular level then you will probably be given a grade within that level, such as 5– or 4+.

Good luck!

Level 4 questions

1 **When a law goes through Parliament it is known as**

   a an act

   b a bill

   c a White Paper.

2 **Which of the following is not a criminal court?**

   a Magistrates Court.

   b Crown Court.

   c High Court.

3 **When a person is on trial in a criminal court, they are known as**

   a the defendant

   b the witness

   c the plaintiff.

4 **When police interview a suspect who is under 17, they must**

   a do so in the presence of an 'appropriate adult'

   b provide refreshments

   c repeat the caution that they issued when the person was arrested.

5 **The age of criminal responsibility means**

   a the age at which a person can be put in prison

   b the age at which a person can be arrested

   c the age at which a person can tell right from wrong.

Level 5 questions

6 **Mary is a witness in a trial that involves theft. Which of these questions is likely not to be allowed if the prosecuting lawyer asks them?**

a 'Is it true that you're very short-sighted?'

b 'Why did you take so long to tell the police?'

c 'You know that she's a thief, don't you?'

7 **Look at the following list of rights. Which one is a civil rather than a human right?**

a The right to a fair trial if arrested.

b The right to receive education until you are 18.

c The right not to be tortured.

8 **Which of the following statements is true?**

a Magistrates are all unpaid and try indictable offences.

b Magistrates are usually unpaid and try summary offences.

c Magistrates are usually unpaid and try indictable offences.

9 **Jim decides to go into his local bank to steal some money. He takes a shotgun which isn't loaded. When he gets there he finds the bank is shut, but the police, acting on information, are waiting for him. The crime that has been committed is**

a attempted robbery

b attempted burglary.

c No crime has been committed.

10 **The police stop Jamie in the street and search him. They tell him that they are searching for drugs and are able to do this because**

a they have reason to believe that he was carrying banned substances at that time

b several people in the area have been caught before with banned substances

c they heard there was a drugs problem at his school.

Level 6 questions

11 **Kelly, who is 16, has been questioned at the police station. She was seen taking a purse from an old lady, and the purse was found on her person. One year ago, she was found guilty of assaulting another girl and was given a final warning. The police will have to**

a give her a second final warning

b send her home and tell her not to offend again

c charge her so that she will appear in court.

12 **Jean walks out of a pub with Richard's umbrella, which is very similar to hers. When she gets home she realises the mistake and plans to take the umbrella back. She then notices that she has damaged it. The police suddenly knock at her door, because Richard has already complained that he saw her take the umbrella. Jean is guilty of**

a theft only

b theft and criminal damage

c neither.

13 **Annual crime statistics show that in England and Wales the general crime rate is going down. However, certain types of crime, such as fraud and Internet crime, are on the increase. This is most likely to be because**

a criminals are becoming lazy, and there are not so many banks to rob

b criminals are getting more used to technology and people carry less cash around.

c criminals are getting more used to technology and getting bored with old methods

14 **We are told by official government statistics that the general crime rate is going down, yet newspapers still suggest that crime rates are getting worse and that the streets are more dangerous than they have ever been. This is least likely to be because**

a the government publishes figures in the best possible way so that they look like they are being successful in fighting crime

b many crimes go unreported and it is not always possible to see the total picture

c newspapers are deliberately trying to frighten people.

15 **The Crown Prosecution Service was set up so that the people who charge criminals (the police) are different to the people who actually prosecute criminals in court. This is most likely to be because**

a it makes sure that the trial will be as fair as possible

b it gives more jobs to people involved in the law

c it is cheaper to do it this way.